TRADING

by Sara Silver
illustrated by Barbara Vagnozzi

SCHOOL PUBLISHERS

Printed in China

ISBN 10: 0-15-351450-7
ISBN 13: 978-0-15-351450-0

Ordering Options
ISBN 10: 0-15-351213-X (Grade 3 Advanced Collection)
ISBN 13: 978-0-15-351213-1 (Grade 3 Advanced Collection)
ISBN 10: 0-15-358086-0 (package of 5)
ISBN 13: 978-0-15-358086-4 (package of 5)

4 5 6 7 8 9 10 0940 12 11 10 09

Emma jumped up as soon as she heard the car engine, threw open the door, and hurried down the steps. "Dad, you're finally home!" she exclaimed as he gave her a big hug.

Emma skipped up the steps. Her father had been away on business for a week, and she had missed him terribly.

"Can we play basketball after dinner?" she asked eagerly.

He chuckled. "I'll try, but I just had an extremely long flight so you might have to give me a few points."

"Where's your Mom?" Dad asked as he started to unpack his briefcase.

"She's in her office," replied Emma.

"Oh, I nearly forgot, Emma, here's something for you," said Dad.

He handed Emma a folded up piece of paper, and when she opened it up she saw an e-mail address and a street address in San Diego.

Emma looked up. "Who is Ashwin Kela?"

"I met his mother at a meeting, and we thought you two might enjoy writing to each other," Dad replied.

4

"Ashwin is nine years old like you, and until last June, he lived in Delhi, but now he lives in San Diego, California," Dad continued.

Emma ran upstairs to her room and switched on her computer.

Hello Ashwin,

My name is Emma. Our parents met and thought we'd like to write because you lived in India and now live in the United States. I lived in San Francisco, California. This fall, my family moved to Bangalore, India. We are the reverse of your family!

Please write back!

Emma

Emma sent the e-mail, and the next day she found a reply.

Hi Emma,

Thanks for writing! I like it here, but San Diego is very different from Delhi. Here it is always sunny, and you can get to the ocean in minutes! Delhi is a huge, busy, noisy city, and it can be crazy, but it is also fun. If you go there to visit, I will tell you what to do and see.

I miss my friends, and I also miss cricket, my favorite sport!
Ashwin

Emma quickly wrote back.

Dear Ashwin,

Everyone here loves cricket! It doesn't make any sense to me. It looks like a cross between baseball and croquet. My favorite sport is basketball, and I can play any position. I love to watch it, too. People tell me that sometimes they have American basketball games on TV, but they're on early in the morning, which is an odd time to watch a game! Emma

Emma began to look forward to Ashwin's messages. Bangalore was more than a day ahead of San Diego. If she checked before school, sometimes there was a message that Ashwin had just sent. However, for him it was still the night before!

Hello Emma,

For homework, we had to write about a place that is important to us, so I wrote about my old home in Delhi. I like everyone in my class, and my friend Ray is teaching me Spanish. *Buenas noches, mi amiga!* (That means, "Good night, my friend!") Ashwin

Buenos dias, mi amigo!

I am going to an International School, which means that my class is a big mix of people. Some are from here in Bangalore, and some are from the United States, like me. Almost everyone speaks some English, so it has not been hard to get along. Many people in Bangalore also speak a language called *Kannada*. I have learned some of it just by listening. Sometimes I can even translate signs or newspaper headlines. Do you know *Kannada*? If so, please send me some words I should know!

Emma

Dear Emma,

We spoke Hindi in Delhi, so if you go there, say *namaste* (na·ma·stay) for me. (That means "hello.")
Ashwin

Emma began to learn Indian dance, and Ashwin tried surfing. They sent each other pictures of their new hobbies.

Emma came home from school one day, and Mom was on the phone. She looked annoyed when she hung up the telephone. "The car needs repairs," Mom sighed. "I'm trying to get it done before I leave on Friday, but finding someone to do it that quickly is bothersome."

"What's happening on Friday?" asked Emma.

"Oh, I have a meeting in Delhi this weekend, and I think you should come with me!" replied Mom.

On Friday afternoon, Dad dropped Mom and Emma off at the airport. They arrived in Delhi a few hours later and went straight to their hotel.

The din of the traffic woke Emma the next morning. She looked out the window and saw a heaving mass of cars jamming the streets. Horns were beeping, and bicyclists were dodging in between cars.

Emma had made a list of places that Ashwin had mentioned in his e-mails. After Mom's meeting, they visited and photographed each place, and then they flew home two days later.

Emma printed out the pictures the next day. She had a picture of Ashwin's favorite restaurant, and a picture of herself at Ashwin's school. There she was at Jantar Mantar, a giant stone where Ashwin had played. She had pictures of an outdoor market and street signs, and she even had a picture outside Ashwin's old home!

Emma found a big envelope and carefully wrote Ashwin's address. The next day, Dad took it to the post office. A few weeks later, she got an e-mail, and the subject line said "THANK YOU!"

Dear Emma,

I got your photos and I love them! I'm not homesick anymore. San Diego is special to me now, too. That doesn't mean I don't think about Delhi, but your photos helped me see it again. I hope you liked my first hometown!
Ashwin

Emma knew exactly how Ashwin felt. At first, thinking about California had made her unhappy, but now it made her smile.

A few weeks later, Emma got a package from Ashwin. There was Ashwin at Union Square, at the Golden Gate Bridge, at the aquarium, and at the San Francisco Zoo. He had photos of all her favorite places. Emma hung the pictures over her desk, and then wrote:

Ashwin,

Thank you for the pictures of San Francisco! I hope you liked my first hometown, too.

Your friend, Emma